Alan COMBES

United
Here
I Come!

With illustrations by
Aleksander Sot......

For Lynne and Abby

First published in 2008 in Great Britain by
Barrington Stoke Ltd
18 Walker Street, Edinburgh, EH3 7LP

www.barringtonstoke.co.uk

This edition first published 2013

ISBN: 978-1-78112-267-9

Printed in China by Leo

Contents

Chapter 1
Primary School

The very first day at Hawks Meade Primary School my teacher, Mrs Green, sat me next to Jimmy Ford. My name is Jack James. All the kids with names that began with J sat together.

I've sat next to Jimmy since we were both five years old and he was a big lad then. He was tall, wide and clumsy. But the thing that everyone noticed about him most was the size of his hands. They were as big as a man's hands even at Junior School.

In those days Jimmy only had one thing on his mind. That was football. He was mad about the game. He could tell you who was the leading goal scorer, which goal-keeper had saved the most shots and who was going to win the League.

To the other lads Jimmy was a joke because he didn't have a clue about playing football. Whenever we played football at school, Jimmy was last to be picked. He was so clumsy. If the ball was passed to him, he fell over. His feet were so big, he was always tripping over them.

"You'll never make a footballer, but with hands like that you might make a good boxer one day, Jimmy," Mr West said after a games lesson one day.

"I don't want to box, Mr West," Jimmy said, "I want to play football and one day I'll play for United." He was not joking. "United, here I come," he said, and he punched his fist in the air.

We were playing football at the time and it seemed as if Jimmy had made the best joke ever. The game stopped when he said that. At least 10 players rolled over and over on the pitch, laughing till the tears ran down their faces.

But Jimmy just did not know what they were laughing about.

Other kids used to ask me why I stayed friends with Jimmy.

"We're both into the same things," I would tell them, "football, football and football." At least it got a laugh.

Chapter 2
The Best Day of the Week

By the time we got to Secondary School, Sunday was the best day of the week for me and Jimmy. We used to meet up at the playing fields in the park and the two of us would kick a ball about.

We used to play in the penalty area of the men's football pitch. We would take it

in turns to be goalie and striker. We made
out that we were famous players on *Match
of the Day*. And we took it in turns to be the
commentator.

It would go like this. Jimmy would shout:
"And here comes Jack James, beats one man
then another. James shoots for goal from the
edge of the penalty area ..."

As Jimmy, in goal, pushed the ball away, I would add: "What a smashing save. The goalie has turned the ball past the post."

Jimmy was much better as a goalie than as an out-field player. It was the size of those huge hands, you see. When he wore gloves, they looked even bigger. For a big lad, he sure could throw himself about.

On muddy winter days, his mum would shout at him because his gear was so filthy.

"They haven't invented a washing machine that will clean up your football stuff. I have to scrub it with my bare hands," she would say.

"Sorry, Mum," Jimmy would say and look
at me with an angry face as though it was me
to blame.

One Sunday when we were kicking the
ball around, Gary Ward and his friends were
hanging around the playing field. They
turned up just when it was Jimmy's turn in
goal and they started shouting things at us.

"The two most useless footballers in our school," Gary Ward shouted and all his mates laughed. They laughed because they were afraid of Gary. He thought he was Top Man.

Jimmy got nervous in goal because they were laughing at him and he really messed up.

"Look at him. He dives like an elephant," joked Gary.

That was unfair. For a big lad, Jimmy could throw himself around the goal mouth.

Me and Jimmy just said nothing. Until Dave Clark, a little kid with a big mouth, stole the ball when it bounced off a post.

They ran off to the other side of the field with it.

"Come on, we can get 'em," I said to Jimmy.

"Just leave them be," Jimmy said.

How could he say that? He was letting them get away with our only football. Were we just going to let them?

"There are six of them and just two of us," Jimmy said.

"So is that it then?" I asked angrily.

"Yeah! See you in the morning at school." Jimmy shrugged and off he went.

Chapter 3
A New Ball

The next morning at school I said to Gary Ward, "You stole our football. When do we get it back?"

"Sorry, Dave kicked it in the river and that's the last we saw of it," Gary said, with a stupid grin on his face.

I thought of telling Mr West, our games teacher, but Jimmy said, "Leave it. It's got nothing to do with school."

That weekend Jimmy and I went into town to buy a new football. We hadn't got the dosh for a leather one. It would have to be a cheap plastic one.

That Sunday at the playing field, it was very windy. Light as a feather, the new ball was bouncing all over the place. Whoever was in goal had a hard time trying to save it.

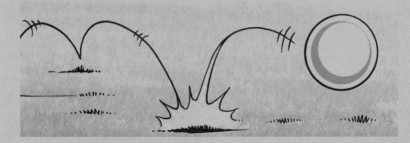

Week after week, all we had was that rubbish plastic ball to play with.

Then two funny things happened. The first thing was that Jimmy got better and better in goal. The new plastic ball seemed to bring out the best in his saving skills. He had to move much faster to get hold of a ball that bounced madly in the wind.

The second thing that happened was that Jimmy got taller and thinner. I suppose it was all a part of growing up.

"That friend of yours, Jimmy Ford, seems to be growing up fast," my mum said to me one day, and she was right.

Because he was taller and thinner, his man-size hands seemed to stand out even more.

Chapter 4
The Champions' Final

In Year 10, Park School were our school's rivals and we were due to play them in the school league for the last game of the season. I was on the bench because Mr West chose me as a sub. Jimmy, of course, was not picked, but he turned up to watch.

It went badly from the start. Gary Ward, the Top Man who stole our football, passed back to Danny Black, the goalie, and it went into our own net. Not even five minutes on the ref's watch and we were 1–0 down.

That was how it stayed until half time. During the break something very bad happened. Mr West had made it a rule that you always took your boots off in the changing rooms.

Danny Black, the keeper, forgot the rule.
He walked across the changing room floor
with slippery studs and fell on his arm.

"Danny, I told you to take your boots off
when you came indoors," Mr West said.

Danny didn't hear a word. He was in
agony rolling over and over on the changing
room floor. We didn't know it then, but his
arm was broken in two places.

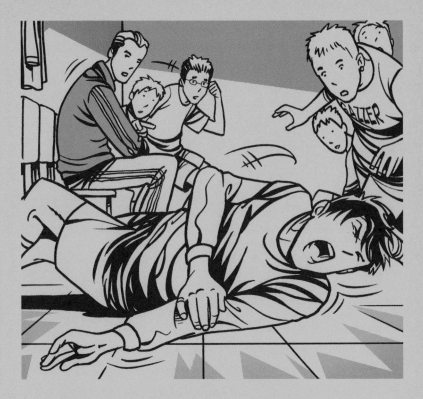

"We're done for," Gary Ward groaned,
"there's no way we will win that
Championship now."

Chapter 5
Jimmy Gets a Game

Everyone in the dressing room was full of gloom because not one of us was any good as a goal-keeper.

Yes, I could come on as a sub. But as a goalie? Never in a million years.

Suddenly I had an idea.

"Mr West, Jimmy Ford is a pretty good goalie," I said.

Half the lads in the team groaned while the other half laughed out loud.

"Are you sure? Jimmy Ford has never even played for the school."

"Sir, he's good. One day he'll be a great goalie."

Then I couldn't help adding, "I play with him every Sunday. He's better than this lot think."

"Well, where is he?"

"He's watching the game on the touch-line."

Mr West spoke to the Park School teacher. Then he called Jimmy into the dressing room. I was amazed.

"We don't have a goalie, so it looks like you're playing for us, Jimmy. You'll have to borrow my top. We don't have one in the kit bag that will fit you."

And that was how I did myself out of a game as sub, but got Jimmy into his first ever match.

Things did not start well. Their striker was a boy named Robbie Blake, who was on trial at Tottenham. He lobbed the ball towards our goal after a corner. Jimmy should have stayed still, but he dived and went right over the ball. It was in the net and we were 0–2 down. Jimmy had acted as if it was the light plastic ball and not a proper leather football. Leather balls move slower.

Everyone looked at me, even Mr West.

Jimmy did not do too badly after that. With five minutes to go, Kevin Kettle got a sneaky goal for us which at least made the score look better. We were only losing 1–2 now.

We got a corner just before the final whistle. Suddenly, like a madman, Jimmy ran upfield and met Gary Ward's corner with his head.

Park's defenders could not believe it. It was as if a thing from outer space had just arrived. The ball flew into the net for 2–2 and we were into a penalty shoot-out.

Me, I was gloating. I punched the air.

Jimmy Ford had just gone from zero to hero.

Now he had a real chance to show them what

he was made of.

Chapter 6
The Penalty Shoot-out

In a shoot-out, as you know, each team takes five penalties. Our captain, Scott Roberts, lost the toss and they chose to take first shot.

Their first penalty-taker was a great shot. He went for the top right hand corner and it was a goal for cert ... until this big meaty fist

came from nowhere and pushed it over the
cross-bar.

"How did he reach that, sir?" Gary Ward
asked Mr West.

Of course, Mr West didn't know, but I did.
I knew how practising with a light plastic ball
brings on your diving skills.

'Top Man' Gary Ward took our first
penalty and he was off target. We could have
been one in front but it stayed at 0–0.

The kid who took their second could
hardly see any space to put the ball in.
Jimmy stood on the goal line like a road-
block. But there was one space – between
Jimmy's legs, and the kid found it.

Luckily, our Kevin Kettle's cool shot made it one–all.

Jimmy saved their third and fourth efforts, flying through the air to left then right.

That should have been that, but our own penalty taking was pathetic. One hit the post and the other landed in their goalie's arms.

1–1, and only one more penalty each.

"Uh-oh, it's that Robbie Blake kid who's on trial at Tottenham. He's taking their last penalty," Mr West said with a lump in his throat.

Blake took a massive run-up, trying to scare Jimmy with the power of his shot. But Jimmy was in mid-air right away and blocked the shot ... with his face. Blood poured from

his nose.

"Cor, for a big lad, he can't half dive," Mr West said.

Big problem. No one on our team wanted to take that last penalty. There was too much at stake. Of course, if I hadn't been on the bench, I would have taken it.

A voice came from the back.

"Mr West, can I take it?"

It was Jimmy.

"How are you going to stop that nose bleeding for long enough to take it?"

They got Jimmy a cold compress which he held in place as he took the spot kick. He swerved to the right at the end of his run-up, the Park goalie dived the wrong way. It didn't matter that it was the worst pen of the afternoon, Jimmy had fooled the goalie, and we had won 2–1 on penalties.

I don't know whether Jimmy enjoyed the next week more than me, but it was great

hearing Gary Ward eat his words. Best of all was when he gave us our old football back; the one he said had floated away down the river.

"Here," he said as he gave it to Jimmy, "you'll be needing this to get in training for United!"

It was meant to be a wind-up, but Jimmy just said, "You'll see."

It was almost as though he knew that his dreams were about to come true.

Chapter 7
United, Here I Come

I thought Jimmy would lose interest in our Sunday afternoon kickabouts once he was school goalie.

"Don't be daft. Using that plastic ball was the best thing we ever did," Jimmy said. "I learned how to dive."

I thought Jimmy would want to be keeper all the time now, but he didn't.

"Got to work on my penalty-taking skills," he would say with a laugh.

One week we saw this old guy watching us. He was taking his dog for a walk. He didn't seem to be at all interested in what his dog was doing. He was too busy watching our kick-about.

He came to watch us for three or four weeks and then one week he turned up without the dog. It was a freezing cold day and he just stood there with his hands in his pockets. At first we didn't see who he was

because he hadn't got the dog with him and he had a baseball cap on his head.

By four o'clock it was getting dark so we packed up to go home. The old guy came over to us.

"Hello, lads, you OK?" He was hard to understand because he spoke with a Scottish accent. "Pretty cold, isn't it?"

"Be dark soon," was all Jimmy said.

"Do you know who I am?" the Scotsman said. Jimmy stayed cool. He just shook his head.

"My name's Don Gibson. Does that mean anything to you?"

"No," me and Jimmy both said.

"I'm the area scout for United," was all he said and my heart jumped a beat.

But I knew it was Jimmy he was after, not me.

"I'd like a talk with your mum and dad, son," he said to Jimmy. "Can I walk home with you?"

"No, I'm not interested," was never going to be Jimmy's answer, was it?

Two weeks later Jimmy went with his mum and dad to United's ground. I saw him after school that evening and he told me he'd signed up for them.

"I met the Manager and all the first team players," he told me in an excited voice.

Just last week Jimmy played for United in the first round of the FA Youth Cup. He even saved a penalty.

When the lads in our school team found out about it, not one of them fell over laughing. They always knew that Jimmy would one day play for United. After all, he'd told them so ... himself.

Our books are tested
for children and young people by
children and young people.

Thanks to everyone who consulted on
a manuscript for their time and effort in
helping us to make our books better
for our readers.

More from *Barrington Stoke*...

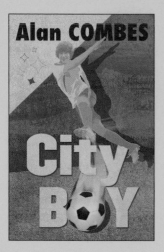

City Boy
ALAN COMBES

Josh loves football – but he needs to get much better to play for City.

His grandad has a plan.

Can he help Josh get to play for his heroes?

The Number 7 Shirt
ALAN GIBBONS

Football is Jimmy's life. When he gets into the Man U Academy, it's a dream come true – but he still has lots to learn. Lucky for him, he's got help... his football heroes.

They all have one thing in common – the Number 7 Shirt. Will Jimmy win now he's got the help he needs?

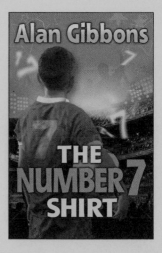

Football Crazy
TONY BRADMAN

Danny and his mates are over the moon when football legend Jock Ramsey agrees to coach their team. For the first time ever the Rovers might have a chance of winning something!

But Ramsey's a tough coach. Can Danny, Lewis and Jamil survive the pressure and stay football crazy – in a good way?

One-Nil
TONY BRADMAN

Luke's best mate's dad works at their local ground and he's let the lads into a big secret – the England team are training there tomorrow!

But Luke knows his mum won't let him have the day off school. And so Luke comes up with a plan to trick his mum. She'll never find out... or so Luke thinks!

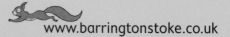

www.barringtonstoke.co.uk